GRANNY GREENTEETH and the NOISE IN THE NIGHT

by Kenn and Joanne Compton
illustrated by Kenn Compton

Holiday House / New York

Printed in the United States of America
First Edition
Library of Congress Cataloging-in-Publication Data
Compton, Kenn.
Granny Greenteeth and the noise in the night / Kenn and Joanne Compton.—1st ed.
p. cm.
Summary: When no one will help Granny find out what's making the noise
under her bed, she starts a chain reaction that brings results.
ISBN 0-8234-1051-X
[1. Noise—Fiction. 2. Night—Fiction. 3. Bedtime—Fiction.]
I. Compton, Joanne. II. Title.
PZ7.C7364Gr 1993 93-18232 CIP AC
[E]—dc20

Deep in the forest, in a creaky old cottage, lived Granny Greenteeth and her old cat.

One night, Granny Greenteeth climbed into bed with her favorite book, a cup of spiderweb tea and her old cat. No sooner had she gotten comfortable when there came a horrible, skin-prickling, hair-raising noise from under her bed.

"Quiet down there!" hollered Granny. "How's a body to read with all that racket going on?"

HOME
SWEET
HOME

But the horrible, skin-prickling, hair-raising noise came again, louder this time. SQUEENK!

"Old cat," snapped Granny, "crawl under this bed and see what's making that horrible, skin-prickling, hair-raising noise that keeps me from my book."

"Not me!" hissed the old cat. "I'll not crawl under a bed with a horrible, skin-prickling, hair-raising noise beneath it. *I'll* not do it."

"HMMPH!" snorted Granny. "We'll see about that." And she clambered out of bed and over to the door.

"Broomstick! Broomstick! Come here and sweep this old cat beneath my bed to find out what's making that horrible, skin-prickling, hair-raising noise that keeps me from my book."

"I don't want to," whined the broomstick. "My back is tired and I need my sleep. Tomorrow is going to be a busy day. *I'll* not do it."

"HMMPH!" snorted Granny. "We'll just see about that." And she marched out of the room and down to the cellar.

"Troll! Troll! Wake up and chase the broomstick so she'll sweep the old cat under my bed to find out what's making that horrible, skin-prickling, hair-raising noise that keeps me from my book."

"Leave me alone," grumbled the troll. "I'm quite comfortable in my cold, damp bed. *I'll* not do it." And he went back to sleep.

"HMMPH!" snorted Granny. "We'll just see about that." And she stomped up the stairs to the hallway.

"Spook, Spook, rattle your chains to wake the troll so he'll chase the broomstick so she'll sweep this old cat under my bed to find out what's making that horrible, skin-prickling, hair-raising noise that keeps me from my book."

"No-o-o!" howled the spook. "My chains will rust in that cold, damp cellar. *I'll* not do it."

"HMMPH!" snorted Granny. "We'll just see about that." And she scurried down the hall to the bathroom.

"Goblin! Goblin! Throw the spook down the stairs so he'll wake the troll so he'll chase the broomstick so she'll sweep this old cat under my bed to find out what's making that horrible, skin-prickling, hair-raising noise that keeps me from my book."

"Not now," whined the Goblin. "I'm polishing my nails and cleaning my toes. *I'll* not do it."

"HMMPH!" snorted Granny. "We'll just see about that." And she climbed the stairs to the attic.

"Black Bats! Black Bats! Fly at the goblin so she'll toss the spook downstairs so he'll wake the troll so he'll chase the broomstick so she'll sweep this old cat under my bed to find out what's making that horrible, skin-prickling, hair-raising noise that keeps me from my book."

"Oh, no!" screeched the bats. "The night is so cold that we don't want to leave our cozy attic rafters. *We'll* not do it."

"HMMPH!" snorted Granny. "We'll just see about that." And she tiptoed over to a large trunk.

"Bugaboo! Bugaboo! Frighten the bats so they'll fly at the goblin so she'll toss the spook downstairs so he'll wake the troll so he'll chase the broomstick so she'll sweep this old cat under my bed to find out what's making that horrible, skin-prickling, hair-raising noise that keeps me from my book."

"No, I'm afraid you've come at a bad time," moaned the bugaboo. "I'm too busy baking teacakes. *I'll* not do it."

"HMMPH!" snorted Granny. "We'll just see about that." Then she stomped three times and shrieked . . .

The bugaboo was so startled that he flew lickety-split back into his trunk and slammed the lid shut . . .

which frightened the bats who flew down from the attic and scared the goblin . . .

who tossed the spook downstairs to the cellar and woke the troll . . .

who chased the broomstick who swept the old cat under the bed to find out what was making that horrible, skin-prickling, hair-raising noise that was keeping Granny Greenteeth from her book.

Out ran a teeny-tiny gray mouse.

“Hah! So this is what was making all that noise? A teeny-tiny gray mouse! Is that what you were afraid of, silly old cat?” chortled Granny. With her handkerchief, she shooed the mouse out of the door.

Granny's cottage was quiet at last. The bugaboo finished baking his teacakes. The bats returned to the attic. The goblin began to polish her nails and clean between her toes. The spook dried his chains and put them away. The troll snuggled deep into his cold, damp bed. The broomstick leaned back into her corner of the hearth. The old cat yawned and settled in for a good night's sleep. And Granny finally got back to her book.

SWEET
HOME

HOME
SWEET
HOME
BLESS THIS HOUSE